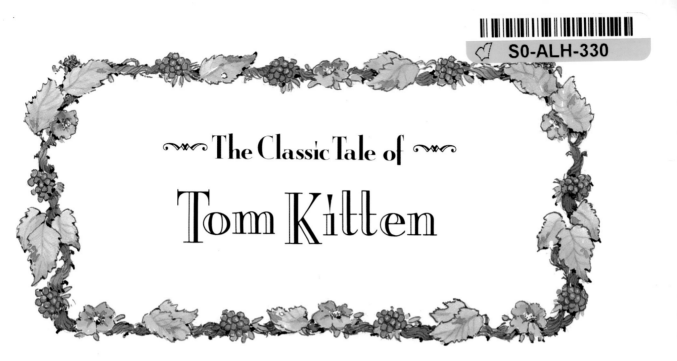

∾ The Classic Tale of ∾
Tom Kitten

Based on the original story by Beatrix Potter

Manufactured in U.S.A.

8 7 6 5 4 3 2 1

ISBN 1-56173-475-6

Cover illustration by Anita Nelson

Book illustrations by T. F. Marsh

Other illustrations by Pat Schoonover

Once there were three little kittens, and their names were Moppet, Mittens, and Tom Kitten. The kittens had beautiful little fur coats, but they liked to tumble about in the yard and play in the dust—they never stayed clean long.

One day, their mother, Mrs. Tabitha Twitchit, expected several of her fine friends for tea. She called her kittens indoors to wash and dress before her company arrived.

First, she scrubbed their faces. Next, she brushed their fur and combed their tails and whiskers. When the kittens were clean, Mrs. Tabitha dressed Moppet and Mittens in fresh dresses.

But for her son Thomas, she took all sorts of handsome—but uncomfortable!—clothes out of the dresser drawers. Tom Kitten had grown fat; three buttons popped off his jacket! His mother sewed them on again.

When the three kittens were ready, Mrs. Tabitha let them out to play while she made hot buttered toast for her tea party. "Now keep your clothes clean, children!" she called. "Keep away from the dirt, Sally Henny-Penny, the pig pen, and most of all, keep away from the Puddle-Ducks."

Moppet and Mittens found it difficult to walk. They tripped on the hems of their dresses and fell on their noses. When they stood up, there were several green stains.

"Let's climb up the rocks, and sit on the garden wall," said Moppet. They turned their dresses back to front, and scampered onto the wall.

Tom Kitten could not jump while wearing trousers. He slowly climbed the rocks by holding onto the ferns. He popped buttons right and left! He was in pieces by the time he reached the top of the garden wall.

Moppet and Mittens tried to pull him together, but his hat fell off, and the rest of his buttons burst. Tom wriggled out of his little coat and trousers. They landed in a heap on the ground.

In the middle of all this trouble, the kittens heard a *pit pat paddle pat!* The three Puddle-Ducks were coming down the road. They were marching one behind the other and doing the goose step, *pit pat paddle pat! pit pat waddle pat!*

The Puddle-Ducks stopped and stood in a row and stared up at the kittens. They had very small eyes, and they looked surprised.

Then, Rebecca and Jemima Puddle-Duck picked up Tom's hat and Moppet's lace handkerchief and put them on!

Mr. Drake Puddle-Duck thought this looked like a good idea. He picked up Tom's suit and put it on himself! "It's a fine morning!" he quacked. The suit fit Mr. Drake even worse than it fit Tom Kitten.

Moppet, Mittens, and Tom Kitten laughed so hard they nearly fell off the wall!

Mr. Drake, Rebecca, and Jemima Puddle-Duck waddled up the road with a *pit pat paddle pat, pit pat waddle pat.* They were a sight!

Mrs. Tabitha Twitchit came down the garden walk and found her kittens wearing none of their fine clothes. She scolded them and dragged them back to the house.

"My friends will arrive in a minute, and you are not fit to be seen. I am embarrassed!" said Mrs. Tabitha Twitchit.

Moppet, Mittens, and Tom were sent up to their room. When her friends arrived, Mrs. Tabitha told them that her little kittens were in bed sick with the measles (which, of course, was not true at all).

Oh, no! Those three little kittens were not in bed: *not* in the least. And Mrs. Tabitha Twitchit's guests heard some *very* strange noises coming from upstairs. The ladies found their quiet tea party to be spoiled.

I think that some day I shall have to write another—longer—book to tell you more about Tom Kitten!

And as for the Puddle-Ducks, they went into a pond. Their clothes all came off, for there were no buttons left to hold them on. Mr. Drake, Rebecca, and Jemima Puddle-Duck have been looking for their fine clothes ever since!